Workshop Roary

First published in Great Britain by HarperCollins Children's Books in 2008

10 9 8 7 6 5 4 3 2

ISBN-10: 0-00-725527-6   ISBN-13: 978-0-00-725527-6

© Chapman Entertainment Limited & David Jenkins 2008

A CIP catalogue record for this title is available from the British Library.

Based on the television series Roary the Racing Car and the original script
'Workshop Roary' by David Ingham.
© Chapman Entertainment Limited & David Jenkins 2008

Visit Roary at: www.roarytheracingcar.com

Printed and bound in Italy by LEGO

Workshop Roary

HarperCollins *Children's Books*

"There's so much more to do before Formula Fun magazine arrive," Big Chris yawned. He had been up all night tidying the workshop. "Mr Carburettor wants the place spotless. But I'm so tired…"

"I'll look after the workshop, while you have a nap," Roary offered.

"Well, if you're sure…" yawned Chris. "Thanks!"

Molecom was trying to make Flash's skateboard go faster.

"OK," he said. "Try it now…"

"It's supposed to go VROOM! VROOM, Molecom, like Maxi," Flash said, miserably.

Maxi arrived at the workshop, coughing. "Has anyone seen Big Chris?" he asked.

"He's having a nap, Maxi," Roary said.

"What?" spluttered Maxi. "He said he'd give me an oil change this morning! I really need one – listen!"

"You're right!" Roary frowned. "I'd better go and wake Big Chris."

"How's Big Chris doing, Rusty?" Roary asked.

"Listen to him snoring!" Rusty replied. "He's sleeping like a Big baby!"

"Oh dear," Roary said. "I can't wake him now. Maxi will just have to wait."

"What do you mean I'll have to wait?" coughed Maxi.

"I'm sure Big Chris will wake up soon," said Roary.

"But if you're in a hurry, we'll do it, won't we, Tin Top?"

But Tin Top didn't look so sure.

Molecom was still trying, unsuccessfully, to improve Flash's top speed. "Now that's what I want to do," exclaimed Flash, as Drifter zoomed by. "That's what I want to sound like!" Suddenly Molecom had an idea. "Well then, let's see if we can borrow an engine from Big Chris. He's bound to have spares!"

Roary had Maxi up on the ramp, ready to change his oil but Drifter had come in with flat tyres.
Roary wasn't sure who to take care of first!
Just then, Flash and Molecom arrived.

o there?" asked Flash

my oil,"

said.

e!"

an

Meanwhile, Marsha was talking to Mr Carburettor.

"Yes, Mr Carburettor," she frowned. "Everything's fine –
I'll check the workshop and the pits, and they'll be spotless...
Yes, of course the cars will look their best... See you soon,
Mr Carburettor. Bye!"

But the workshop wasn't spotless. In fact, it was quite a mess.

"How did this happen?" asked Marsha.

"It's my fault," said Big Chris, walking in on the messy workshop. "I was so tired I left the cars in charge while I had a nap. I'm sorry."

"It's my fault," said Roary. "I promised to wake him if anything needed to be done, but I didn't want to disturb him, so I tried to take care of things myself. I'm sorry."

"I'm sorry, too," said Marsha. "I didn't know you were so tired, Big Chris. But what are we going to do?"

"Well, we all made the mess," said Big Chris. "So we should all clear it up!"

Everyone worked really hard to clear
up the mess. Big Chris changed Drifter's
tyre and filled Maxi up properly with
clean oil. Marsha mopped up all the
oil from the floor and all the cars
tidied up the workshop.

By the time they could hear Mr Carburettor's helicopter approaching, everything was spick and span again!

Molecom had fixed the new engine to Flash's skateboard.

"Let's see what my new souped-up skateboard can do then!" he cried.

"Do be careful, Flash," said Molecom, looking worried. "It will be really quite fast now... Oh dear..."

Mr Carburettor was talking to the reporter. "Yes, Silver Hatch is without doubt the finest racetrack in the world. We have the best workshops, best pits, best mechanic, best marshall…"

Just then, Flash zoomed past!

"… the fastest rabbits…" Mr Carburettor continued without thinking.

"Fastest rabbits?" asked the journalist.

"Yes…" said Mr Carburettor. "Erm, let's take a photograph of me with all the cars, shall we?"

So everyone got together for a group photograph and even Flash got into the picture!

Roary realised that looking after Silver Hatch really was a team effort.

That's why it was the best racetrack in the world – and almost certainly the only one with a flying rabbit!

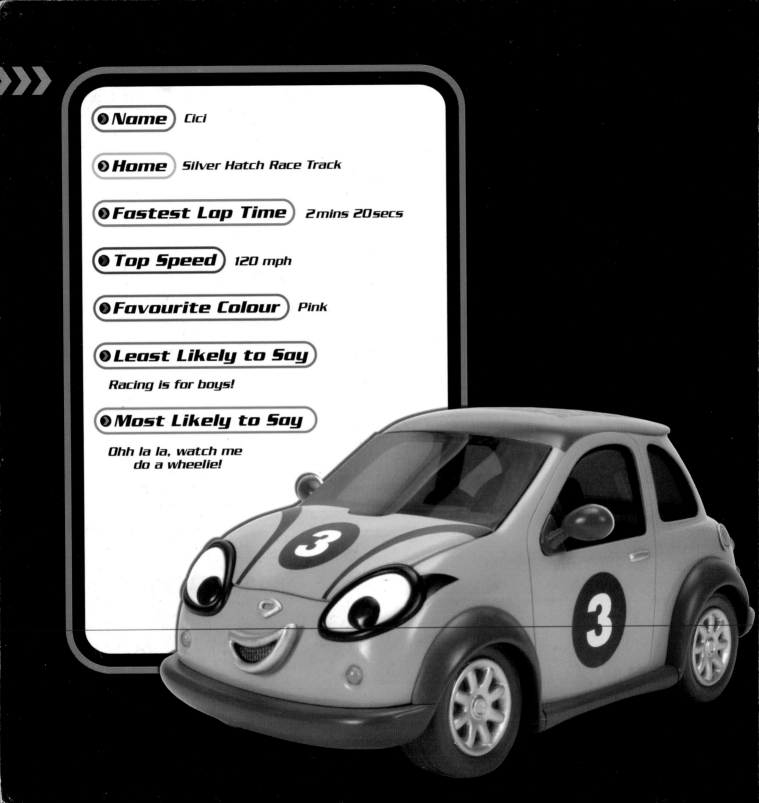

> Name Cici

> Home Silver Hatch Race Track

> Fastest Lap Time 2 mins 20 secs

> Top Speed 120 mph

> Favourite Colour Pink

> Least Likely to Say

Racing is for boys!

> Most Likely to Say

Ohh la la, watch me
do a wheelie!

Cici

Race to the finish line with these fun story and activity books.

Big Chris's Big Workout
Can Big Chris beat Marsha round the track?

Flash Flips Out
Roary's racing and Flash is furious!

Roary's First Day
Can Roary make a splash at Silver Hatch?

Pole Position Poster Book
Customise the cars with Roary!

Big Chris's Race Day Sticker Book
Help Big Chris get Roary ready to race!

Start your engines with Talking Big Chris!

Roary the Racing Car is out soon on DVD!

Rev up R/C Roary to race to victory!

Go Roary, go-oooo!

Get ready to race!

Light 'em up Roary!

DL0742174

Visit Roary at www.roarytheracingcar.com